NiNJA KiD

Scholastic Children's Books
An imprint of Scholastic Ltd
Euston House, 24 Eversholt Street, London, NW1 1DB, UK
Registered office: Westfield Road, Southam, Warwickshire, CV47 0RA
SCHOLASTIC and associated logos are trademarks and/or
registered trademarks of Scholastic Inc.

First published in the US by Scholastic Inc. 2018
First published in the UK by Scholastic Ltd. 2019

Copyright © Anh Do, 2018
Illustrations by Jeremy Ley

The right of Anh Do to be identified as the author of this work has
been asserted.

ISBN 978 1407 19334 2

A CIP catalogue record for this book
is available from the British Library.

Printed by CPI Group (UK) Ltd, Croydon, CR0 4YY
Papers used by Scholastic Children's Books are made
from wood grown in sustainable forests.

1 3 5 7 9 10 8 6 4 2

This is a work of fiction. Names, characters, places, incidents
and dialogues are products of the author's imagination or are used
fictitiously. Any resemblance to actual people, living or dead,
events or locales is entirely coincidental.

www.scholastic.co.uk

ANH DO

illustrated by Jeremy Ley

NiNJA KiD

SCHOLASTIC

ONE

I was super excited about my tenth birthday . . . but it didn't start out great because I opened my eyes to see **this** on my nose.

AAAAA

Spiders are my **worst** nightmare!
I flung it off before it could bite
me and jumped out of bed. My foot
got **stuck** in the blanket, sending
me into an EPIC FALL.

Falling is something I do A LOT.
But this morning, something *very*
strange happened instead.

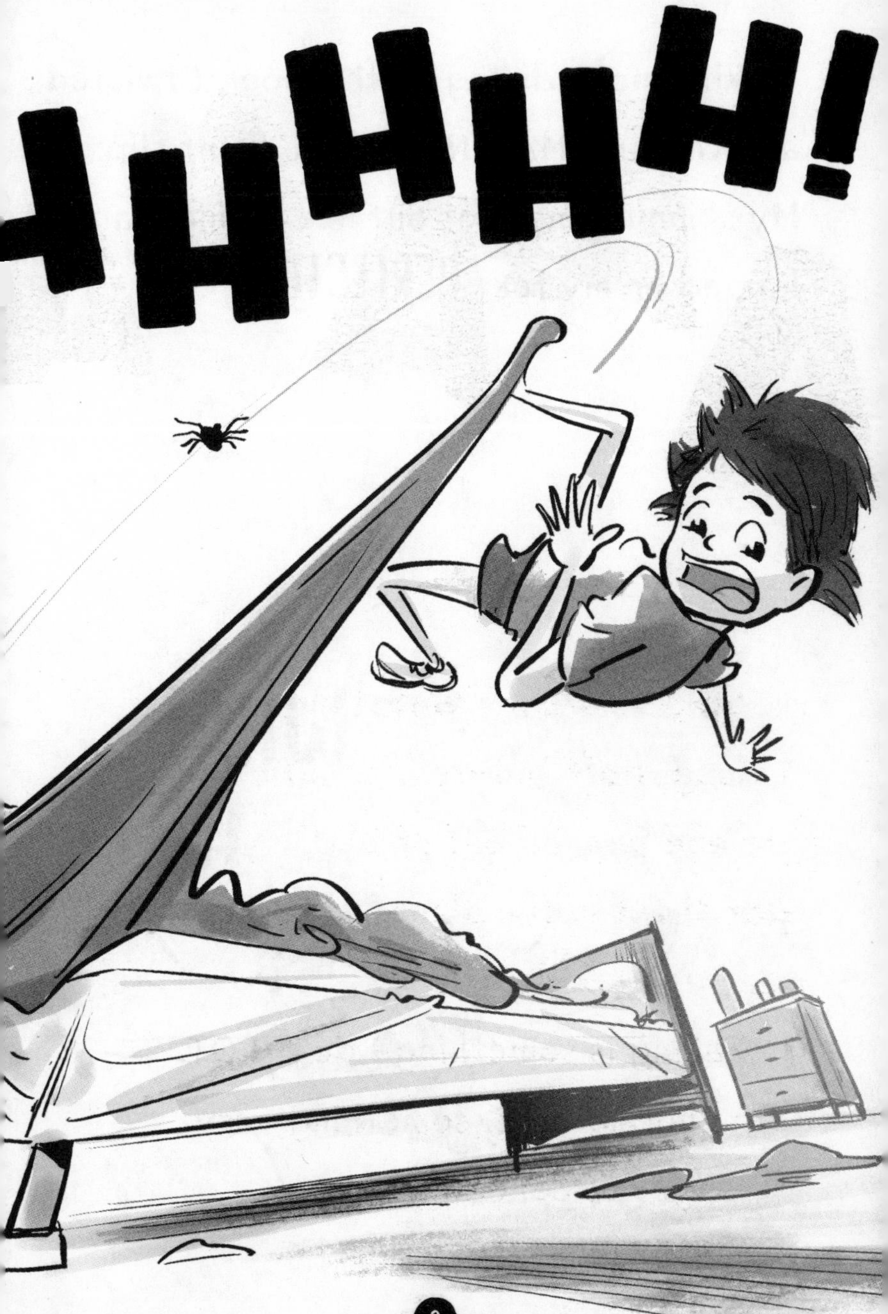
HHHHH!

While nose-diving to the floor, I twisted and did an AMAZING double front flip. My skinny arms shot out like springs, and I landed on my feet **PERFECTLY!**

WHAT THE?!

I am Nelson Kane. **Nerdy** Nelson Kane, who lives in a junkyard in Duck Creek. **Tripping** is something I do. **Falling** is something I do. An amazing double front flip is **NOT** something I do!

Every morning, the mirror reminds me of *exactly* who I am.

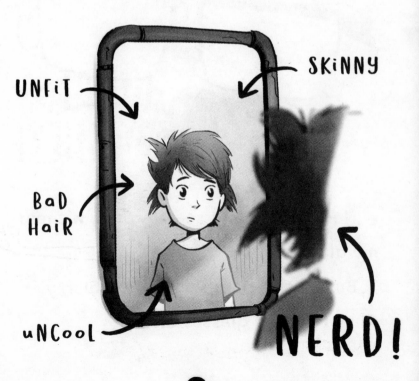

UNFIT

SKINNY

BaD HaiR

uNCool

NERD!

But this morning, when I looked in the mirror, I noticed that something *else* was very strange . . . I could see myself perfectly . . . **without** my glasses!

Normally, I can't see *anything* without my glasses.

But on this day, things went blurry when I put my glasses **ON!**

Took them off . . . clear.

HUH?

What was going on?!

"Nelson! Breakfast!" called my mum
from downstairs.

I rubbed my eyes. Maybe I was still
dreaming when I did that awesome flip?

But how could I explain my perfect
eyesight?

"Happy birthday, Nelson!" shouted
Mum, Grandma Pat and Cousin Kenny
from the kitchen.

They were standing at the table with a **HUGE** chocolate birthday cake.

Mum handed me a present that looked like it'd been wrapped in the same paper she used at Christmas.

We live in a **junkyard**, and it isn't doing very well, so Mum has to work hard as a cleaner to make ends meet. That's why she tries to save money where possible.

I carefully unwrapped the old paper.
Not one but **two** brand-new
Superhero sweaters!

COOOL!

They were special ones with hoods that
came all the way down past your eyes, so
you looked just like a **real** superhero!

Right away, I pulled one on.
Oh man . . . they were nice, but they
were **waaaaay** too big for me!

"They were the only sizes left on the two-for-one discount rack," Mum explained. "You'll grow into them."

"I love them!" I said, thinking it might take me **five years** to grow into them!

"And don't forget **my** present," said Cousin Kenny. He handed me a packet of cookies, tied with a ribbon.

"Awesome," I said, "my favourite!"

I pulled off the ribbon and the packet was empty, except for a note that said, **"I OWE YOU."**

"I was **really** hungry," said Kenny.

Cousin Kenny is skinny, but man, can he eat!

"No problem, Kenny. I know how much you love chocolate cookies. Thanks anyway."

Then Grandma handed me a tattered-looking backpack.

"You're a big boy now, Nelson, and you're going to need some big-boy stuff," she said. "Go ahead . . . look inside."

I unzipped the backpack and pulled out a bunch of weird things. One device looked really **strange!**

"What's this?"

"It's a **torch** and a **heater** rolled into one!"

"That's **Super** neat!" said Kenny. "For when it's dark *and* cold!"

"Thanks, Grandma!" I said.

My grandma is really cool. While other grandmas sit around knitting socks, mine invents awesome stuff . . . sort of. I say "sort of" because she mostly makes **weird** contraptions.

It's handy the junkyard is
filled with old stuff to use.

From broken-down lawn mowers to old cars and computer junk.

OPEN

17

Grandma spends all day taking machines apart to make **new** things.

Grandma's inventions are brilliant and might have made us a lot of money, if it weren't for the fact that they sometimes work, and sometimes DON'T.

Like the amazing solar-powered running shoes. On a sunny day, these shoes can help you run **super fast!**

Only problem is, when a cloud comes along and blocks the sunlight . . . the shoes go **backward!**

Or the motorized bike that runs on
bananas. Environmentally friendly, easy
on the legs . . .

Only problem is, after a while you start to **smell** like bananas. I found this out the hard way when I rode past the monkeys at the zoo.

Then there's the microwave clothes dryer that dries clothes in ten seconds flat. Who wouldn't want one of those? Thing is, Grandma's supersonic dryer occasionally **shrinks** shorts from a size twenty to a **size two!**

OUCH!

And that gave me a **great** idea!

"Guys!" I said. "We can make my sweaters shrink in Grandma's supersonic dryer!"

"Good thinking!" said Kenny.

"OK," said Grandma nervously. "I might have to make a few adjustments . . . don't want to ruin the sweaters. Luckily there's **two** of them!" she joked.

TWO

Be careful out there, guys!" said Mum. "Remember to wear your glasses, Nelson."

"I don't need them any more," I mumbled.

Mum froze.

"What?!"

"Yeah, when I woke up this morning . . . my eyesight was perfect . . ."

Mum looked nervously across at Grandma.

"Oh my!" gasped Grandma.

"Has . . . anything ELSE happened today?" asked Mum.

Now they were **both** staring at me strangely.

"Like what?" I said. "What do you mean?"

"Do you feel **different** today ... or have you noticed anything else unusual?" Mum asked.

What was she talking about? Did she KNOW that so far this had been the **weirdest day of my life?**

"Maybe," I replied. "I did this crazy front flip across my room this morning."

Mum turned straight to Grandma.
They looked at each other like this
wasn't weird at all. Like this was exactly
what they thought I was going to say!
But how could they know?!

HUH?!

Mum took a deep breath and put her arm around me.

"We have something to tell you, Nelson," she said. "We were waiting to see if anything would change today – on your tenth birthday – and it seems it has."

Mum's voice sounded so serious, even Kenny stopped eating just to listen!

"Nelson," said Mum, "legend predicts that a young ninja's skills will surface on the day he turns ten."

A young NINJA?! What was she talking about?!

"Your dad was the last ninja on earth," she added, "and since he's no longer with us . . . I believe **you** are now the last ninja on earth."

Whaaat?

My head was spinning.

What was going on?

"**COOOOL,**" Kenny squealed. "You're a ninja, Nelson! That means you can jump over things backward!"

"**No, I can't!**" I shrieked. "You're all crazy. This morning was a total accident!"

"Why don't you try something?" said Grandma, pushing out her chair. "Right now. Try jumping backward over this."

No way!

I imagined myself jumping back and crashing right through the table. That would show them I was the same old **nerd** I was yesterday, and definitely not some awesome **ninja**.

"Come on!" Kenny urged, clapping excitedly.

"OK. Here goes," I said.

I bent my knees and leaped!

Exactly as I expected, I leaped all crooked, bumped the chair, and **tripped!**

My foot yanked the tablecloth right off the table!

"The cake!" Kenny yelled, and I realized I'd sent it flying up in the air.

Suddenly, in my mind, everything went into slow motion. Before I hit the ground, I twisted into a reverse roll, reached forward . . . and caught the cake perfectly with my foot.

"**WOW!**" said Kenny. "You just saved the cake! You should be a baker!"

CLINK!

CLINK!

"Nelson's not a baker, Kenny," said Mum. "He's a **ninja**."

"A ninja who saves **food** from destruction!" said Kenny. "The best type of ninja!"

Grandma looked at the cake . . . and all the stuff on the ground. "You've got a long way to go before you know how to use your skills properly," she said, "and I'm here to help. But your mum's right. There is no doubt about it, Nelson . . . **you are a NINJA!**"

"Whoa," I murmured. "You're saying I'm a ninja . . . and my dad was a ninja, too? But I thought Dad was a fisherman who got lost at sea?"

Mum and Grandma looked awkwardly at each other.

"Your dad," said Grandma, "was **the greatest ninja who ever lived**. But . . . as he discovered, being a ninja doesn't make you invincible. In fact, it can be very dangerous—"

"Son," interrupted Mum, taking my hand, "it is your destiny to help and protect all the people of the world from the forces of evil. But right now, I need you to **eat your breakfast**."

Protect the world?!

Me?

A ninja kid?

Yesterday I spent the whole day with my **underpants on backward**.

I really don't think I'm ready for this.

THREE

Grandma Pat's workshop was at the back of the junkyard, right between the broken TVs and a **HUGE** mountain of old tires. Grandma spent hours in there, tinkering away on **gizmos**, trying to make cool stuff for us to sell.

Kenny and I had to weave our way
through old strollers and kitchen sinks to
get there. It wasn't easy for Kenny, who

was carrying a plate with a **massive** slice of birthday cake. He'd already eaten two whopping pieces but insisted on bringing "just one more" with him.

"I get hungry when I'm working," he explained with a shrug.

Thing is, Kenny doesn't do any *working* in the workshop. But he does do a lot of talking, joking and **eating**.

My feet seemed to be moving much **faster** than normal, and I was even able to **leap** over tall piles of junk without stumbling once! Normally I'd run out of breath just **walking** to the workshop.

Could this ninja talk be true? Surely these powers had been given to the **wrong kid!**

There were all sorts of buzzing noises coming from inside the workshop.

We pulled open the sliding doors and found Grandma hunched over something. It was the microwave clothes dryer, only now it seemed to have a long hose with a nozzle attached on the end.

"Hello, boys." She jerked the nozzle back, and a blue laser beam suddenly shot out with a loud **bang**. "Duck!" she yelled.

The beam was heading straight for Kenny! My arms **darted** out faster than ever before and I pulled Kenny out of the way. The laser hit his plate of food instead.

ZAP!

DUCK!

"Hey, where'd my cake go?" said Kenny.

Suddenly, we heard a sound like a coin dropping. I looked down to the floor and there was the plate of cake . . . only it had shrunk to the size of a **grape!**

"Well, what do you know, my **ZAP-O-MATIC** works!" cried Grandma.

"What about my cake?!" yelled Kenny.

But then he began to smile. "Grandma, I need to borrow this machine the next time I have to eat brussels sprouts!"

Grandma showed us the nozzle on the machine that could make things ten times **smaller**, or ten times **bigger**.

I hung my sweaters on a rack. Grandma adjusted the nozzle, aimed at them, and **fired!**

The sweaters instantly shrank to the perfect size! I pulled one back on and gave Grandma a high five.

"I have some other **cool stuff** to show you," said Grandma. "Follow me."

Grandma led us to the far wall of the workshop. She stopped and looked at it with a big grin. I could see nothing there but dust and a few cobwebs.

"Um, *really* cool wall, Grandma," said Kenny sarcastically. "We've never seen a **WALL** before."

"Boys," said Grandma, smirking. "I don't think you *have* seen one of these before."

And with that, she pressed a bunch of bricks in sequence. Before our eyes, the wall began **MOVING!** **What the?!**

Behind it was a dark passage.

Grandma stepped into the darkness.

"Well, what are you waiting for?"
she called. "Come on into . . . my **secret**
workshop!"

The inside was filled with **amazing** high-tech devices. There were silver shoes, a bionic glove, and laser beams of all shapes and sizes.

I couldn't believe what I was seeing!

"Where are we?!" asked Kenny.

"We're inside the tires," Grandma explained. "I started working on this place years ago. Dug a tunnel into the tire mountain and built this – a top secret place to protect my most important inventions and training equipment. All of this has been waiting for **you**, Nelson!"

"For me?" I said.

All of this was for me?!

Was I dreaming?

"OOOUCH!"

Kenny **pinched** me hard on my elbow!

"I could tell you thought you were dreaming," said Kenny. "But you're **awake**."

"I'll do whatever I can to help you," said Grandma. "If I were a ninja, I would teach you ninja skills. But I'm not, I'm an inventor, so **THIS** is what I have to help you fulfil your destiny."

I reached out for some funny-looking gloves.

"You're not quite ready for those," said Grandma.

"We'll have to work up to this stuff. First things first."

Grandma leaned over and tapped my bag. "This is **no ordinary backpack**, Nelson. It powers the devices that you're going to need."

I looked at the backpack and noticed some small electrical sockets.

This was crazy.

"No way, Grandma, this is nuts," I said. "I can't do this. **I can't be a ninja kid!** I'm the weakest person I know! How am I supposed to help anyone?"

"You can, Nelson! A person's strength lies not in their muscles, but **up here!**" She tapped her head.

"And you are **very strong** up here,
Nelson."

She continued, quite serious now, "People
often give up too early, not realizing they
can unlock great power when they keep on
trying. And trying comes from inside of
you."

I guess she could be right. Grandma was certainly a person **who kept on trying**.

She grabbed the backpack. "You might not get it the first time, but you just have to pick yourself up and try again. That's the only way to learn! Look at my inventions – they **hardly ever** work the first time."

Grandma connected a laser beam to the side of the pack. The nozzle fell off and **crashed** to the floor.

"Oops! It just needs a little more
sticky tape."

Just then, Kenny pressed a button on the corner of the pack.

A pair of chopsticks came flying right at me!

I jumped out of the way just in time.

"**Sorry!**" said Kenny. "That was close!"

Grandma pulled out a small box and handed it to me.

"This box contains the most important items a ninja student needs," she said.

"What are they?" I asked.

"Plasters."

FOUR

The next morning, I got up and went to find Mum. She never talked about my dad much, and I wanted to learn more.

"What was he like?" I asked her.

"He had really messy hair . . . and he often forgot to brush his teeth . . . but he had these lovely brown eyes . . . and his ears were big but soft . . . and he–"

"No, Mum," I said, "I mean, what was his **personality** like?"

"Oh, yes, of course! He was brave and clever and kind – a lot like you, Nelson."

"I'm not brave, Mum. I'm really scared I'll fail."

"Bravery is feeling scared but having the **courage** to go ahead and do what's right anyway. That's how your dad became **a great ninja**. You know, he wasn't great right away; he had to learn."

"Really?" I said, surprised.

"Of course, and he was scared of failure, too, but he learned to be **brave**."

That was that. If my dad was brave . . . well, I wanted to be like that, too. I woke Kenny up and dragged him out to train.

We met Grandma in the junkyard, where she was standing next to a huge barrel.

About thirty feet away was a row of empty cans on a table.

It was day two of my new life as a ninja, but I still felt **way** more NERD

than NINJA!

Be positive, I thought to myself. *Maybe today's training session will change all that!*

Grandma tapped the side of the barrel. "This *used to be* my collection of old paint can lids," she said. "But now they're MUCH cooler!"

"These are **ninja discs**," said Grandma, "and this morning we're going to work on **MIND POWER!**"

My mind works pretty well when it comes to maths or spelling . . . but flinging sharp objects at faraway targets? I don't think so!

"Cool," said Kenny as he unpeeled a banana. I was pretty sure it was his fifth one already.

"Target practice! Let's see what you can do!" said Grandma.

I picked up one of the discs and wondered what Grandma had done to make these **the perfect ninja gadgets**.

"Do these ninja discs have a built-in GPS?" I asked.

"Ahhh, no. They're just can lids," said Grandma. "Nothing fancy. Sometimes the greatest creation to use is your own mind and body. *You'll* be the guide for these."

I needed to use **my own skill?!** But the targets were so far away . . . I had ZERO chance of hitting one!

"Just give it a try," said Grandma.

"You have to start somewhere."

"OK," I said. "Here goes . . ."

FLING!

"**Duck!**" yelled Grandma.

My first attempt flew completely sideways to my **RIGHT** and sliced the top off Kenny's banana!

HUH!

"**Hey!** I was eating that!" he shrieked. Kenny groaned and moved to my left.

Grandma handed me another disc and nodded again.

I took a deep breath, and **FLING!**

"**DUCK!**" yelled Grandma.

This time, my ninja disc flew sideways to the **LEFT**, lopping off another slice of Kenny's banana.

"**Hey!** What are you trying to do, make fruit salad?" yelped Kenny.

"Sorry, Kenny," I said. Man, I was terrible! I was **dangerous** for all the wrong reasons!

"Take your time, Nelson," said Grandma. "Just imagine exactly where you want your disc to go . . . and then make it happen. You have to **believe** you can do it."

I took another deep breath and told myself, I can do this. I can do this. **I CAN do this.**

I pictured the disc slicing through the air and into the first can in the line.

FLING!

TING!

I got it! The disc struck the first can right in the middle, just like I wanted it to.

"**Woo-hoo!**" Grandma shouted.

"That was **awesome!**" said Kenny. "Do it again!"

"Here goes!" I scooped up a handful of ninja discs and took aim.

FLiNG!

TiNG! PiNG

Got it!

FLING!

Missed!

WHOOOOOSHH

FLING! FLING! FLING!

Missed! Missed!

SWHING

PLOK

Got it!

83

It took ages and ages, but slowly I got better. The last five cans I hit **five times in a row!**

Grandma grinned. "Good work, Nelson. See what practice can do? You boys better be on your way to school," she added. "Don't you have some nature trip today?"

"Sure do," said Kenny. "That's why *my* backpack's filled with **BUG OFF** repellent!"

Kenny **hated bugs and spiders** almost as much as I did. Neither of us was excited about hanging out in the woods today. I'd much rather have been going to

the museum.

Kenny would much rather have been
going to an **all-you-can-eat buffet**.

Grandma handed me my new backpack.
"Meet me here again tomorrow morning.
We have a lot more work to do."

FiVE

The bus dropped off Kenny and me at the start of the forest walk. Soon, other kids from school arrived.

I liked most of the people from my school. We were all just a bunch of kids trying to get by.

Sarah was really nice. I liked her because she treated everyone the same. Sometimes she even said **hi** to me.

"Hi, Nelson," said Sarah.

"Hi, Sarah," I said back.

Sarah walked off to join her friends.

And then the moment I dreaded – a huge black BMW came around the corner, grunting like an **angry rhino**, and stopped as everyone turned to stare. The driver got out wearing his little hat and white gloves, and opened the door for **Charles Brock**.

Charles Brock. Son of Mayor Brock. **The richest kid in Duck Creek**. There's nothing wrong with rich kids. I mean, I'd love to be a rich kid, too, but this guy just rubbed everyone's noses in it.

When Charles stepped out of the car, he spotted me first . . .

"Hey, Nelson . . .

you got new

threads!" he said.

I turned to walk away.

"That's a **cool** sweater!" he added.

Wow, what was he saying? Maybe he was being nice today? The thing about Charles was that sometimes he **was** really nice. That's why he was so popular.

I nodded. "Thanks."

Charles reached out to pat me on the shoulder. Or so I thought . . . Instead, he **grabbed** at something.

"Looks like your mum's been shopping at the **thrift store** again!" Charles laughed and showed everyone the **SALE** tag I'd left hanging from my new hoodie!

Oh man... How was I supposed to save the **world** from evil forces when I couldn't even stop this guy from making fun of me?

Charles Brock's insults don't even bother me that much. It's just that lots of kids think he's cool and they laugh along. Mostly because his dad's the mayor and he always has the latest iPad or iWatch or whatever.

Charles has buddies who follow him everywhere. They came over to laugh as I tried to **rip** the tag off my hoodie.

Kenny quickly rushed over. **"Somebody better hold me back!"** he yelled.

Kenny always says that.

It's my cue to **hold him back**. He started punching the air, making windmills with his fists as I held him.

"You're lucky my cousin's here to stop me!" screamed Kenny. "Otherwise, you'd be in big trouble!"

"You two should crawl back to your junkyard," sneered Charles.

"**Come on, class!**" Mr Fletcher called out. "The trail awaits."

Charles smirked at us and walked away.

Kenny wiggled out of my arms. "Stupid bully," he muttered. "Just wait till he finds out you're **a ninja — the last ninja on earth!**"

I clamped my hand over Kenny's mouth.

SHH!

"Shhhh, no one's supposed to know about that!" I whispered.

And, I felt like saying, *I'm a* **lousy ninja** *anyway. A ninja who can't even stand up for himself!*

Kenny pulled my hand away and pointed above us.

"Look at that! It looks like a massive spiderweb!"

Above us was some weird white stuff hanging between the tops of the trees.

"Nah, Kenny, it's **way** too big
to be a spiderweb."

"Yeah, you're right," he laughed.

"If that was a spiderweb,
the spider would have to be

the size of a **DUMP TRUCK!**"

I laughed, too, but something about that weird white stuff made me feel nervous.

Our class was heading up the trail when I noticed some **strange** ripples in the distant treetops.

"Can you **see** that?" I whispered to Kenny.

"See **what?**"

"The trees."

"The trees? Yes, I can see many trees, Nelson. It's because we're in *the woods*."

"They're moving funny," I said.

Kenny looked at me like I was crazy.

"What about that high-pitched **ringing?** Can you hear that?" I added.

"Nope," said Kenny.

Something strange was happening ahead of us. I could **feel** it.

"Hey, I don't want to scare anyone,"

I called out, "but there **MIGHT** be something weird going on ahead."

"Yeah, right," scoffed Charles. "I think that discount sweater is so tight it's affecting your brain!"

Suddenly . . .

103

A **GIGANTIC** spider appeared out of nowhere!

Everyone started **screaming** . . . even the teacher.

I completely froze. **THIS** was my worst nightmare.

Kenny shook me.

"Nelson – don't worry! I came prepared!" Kenny said. He reached into his bag and pulled out his secret weapon. **"BUG OFF!** Max strength!"

The giant spider made its way towards us. It was HUGE!

Its teeth were the size of **big daggers!**

"Hey, guys!" yelled Kenny. "This should keep that hairy thing away!"

Kenny started **spraying** us all, passing the can around. Just when Sarah started using it, Charles **snatched** it out of her hands and completely covered himself with spray.

Along with all the screaming, I thought
I could hear a strange whipping noise . . .
WHUP-WHUP-WHUP-WHUP . . .
What was that?

It was quickly getting louder and
louder and within moments a red
helicopter thundered above us.

A menacing voice on a megaphone
boomed through the air . . .

"You think **insect repellent** is going to protect you? My Tyranno-Spider **EATS** insect repellent for breakfast!"

A Tyranno-Spider? What was going on? Who was that voice?

The Tyranno-Spider headed straight for Charles, who was **dripping** with BUG OFF.

The voice was right – this giant, crazy spider LOVED insect repellent!

The spider **shot** a thick web at Charles and began **spinning** him in layers of silk.

AHH!

Everyone went **totally nuts** and started running off into the forest.

Everyone but me.

"Let's go!" yelled Kenny, tugging on my arm. **"Come on!"**

But I couldn't. I stood completely still. I kept thinking about what my mum had told me yesterday. That it was my destiny to protect ALL the people of the world . . . even a **bully** like Charles Brock.

I darted for the can of BUG OFF that was lying near the spider's feet.

"Just let the spider take him!" Kenny yelped. "We'll be doing Duck Creek a favour!"

"I have to do the right thing, Kenny!" I shouted. "It's my duty to protect people. **Even** people like Charles."

"That stinks!" said Kenny.

"I know. **Over here, spider!**" I yelled.
"I've got a **whole** can of **BUG OFF!**"

HEY!

I started spraying up into the air.

The spider instantly **sniffed** the spray and turned towards me, dropping Charles to the ground.

"Kenny! Get Charles back to the bus!"

"Do I have to?"

"YES!"

The spider jumped towards me.

AAAHHH!

I ran faster than I ever had before, skipping across rocks and leaping over logs. The spider raced after me, scaling up and down trees along the way.

The forest flew past in a blur and suddenly I realized I was heading straight for **a cliff!** I twisted and skidded to a stop just in time!

Over the edge was a great ravine and a raging river.

I was trapped. The Tyranno-Spider was getting closer!

"Come on, ninja instincts! **Kick in!**"

I could barely breathe, I was so exhausted, and the spider was almost on top of me. Some ninja I was turning out to be!

BING! I suddenly had a great idea! If I threw the bug spray off the cliff, the spider might go over the edge after it.

I tossed the can as hard as I could but it got stuck in a branch!

CLUNK!

Oh man!

And then something grabbed my ankle. The spider had wrapped its web around my leg. It was pulling me towards its **sharp teeth!**

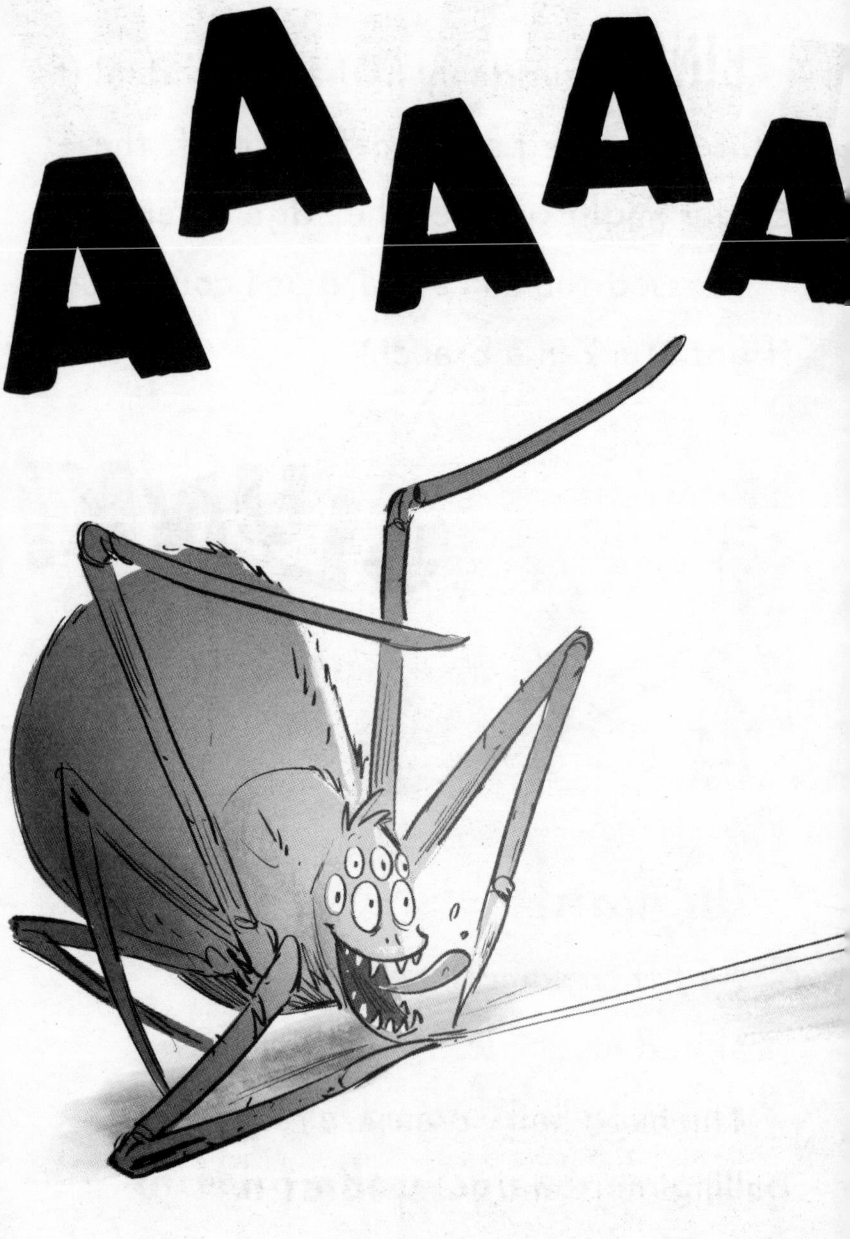
AAAAA

The huge hairy creature reared up on its hind legs and **jumped at me!**

A split second before impact, I rolled to the left and stretched out my leg so that the spider's fangs would **cut** through the web that was trapping my ankle.

SLICE!

It worked! I scrambled to my feet and darted behind a boulder.

"*You are a ninja,*" I whispered. **"You ARE a ninja."** I looked around and saw a small, round purple rock.

I picked it up, aimed carefully . . . and flung it at the BUG OFF can.

The purple rock sliced into the can and it fizzled and tumbled down into the ravine. The spider's eyes glowed red, and it scurried after the can, right off the **cliff** . . .

The spider tumbled after the can, all the way down to the wild river below.

"No, Tyranno-Spider!" the voice from the chopper boomed. "No time to chase breakfast, we have work to do!"

The helicopter went after the spider and I ran back to the bus.

"That was one hairy situation," yelled
Kenny as he pulled me inside. **"Driver,
step on it! Let's get out of here!"**

SiX

Mum and Grandma rushed to us as soon as we got home. They'd heard all about the **giant spider** on the news.

CLASSIFIED

The story was everywhere!

"Are you two OK?" asked Mum, checking us over.

"We're fine," I said.

"Nelson," said Grandma, "did he **see** you?"

"The spider?!"

"No, not the spider . . ."

"The guy flying the chopper?" I asked. "I don't think so. I mean, I was wearing my hood – it covers half my face . . ."

Mum gave Grandma an odd look. **"Why? Who is he?"** I asked worriedly.

"Let's go talk in the workshop," said
Grandma.

We all sat at a long desk in Grandma's
secret headquarters. In front of us was
a wall of screens made from old TVs and
computers.

"Your father was a great ninja,
Nelson," started Grandma.

"What happened to him?" I asked.

For as long as I could remember, I'd always pictured Dad in a small fishing boat, drifting into a dark storm . . . and being swallowed by the sea.

But Thomas Kane, my dad, was a ninja. And I was about to find out the **truth**.

"Your dad went out on a ninja mission one day," Grandma explained. "Like he'd done thousands of times before. But on this day ... **he never came back**."

"You were so little," said Mum. "It was really hard. Grandma and I tried to find out what happened, but we could never get any answers. Your dad just **vanished** without a trace."

"I think I know who is responsible for your dad's disappearance," said Grandma. "A **brilliant** young man who *could* have become **a great scientist.**"

Grandma took a deep breath . . .

"I was his mentor. Back when I was a professor, he was my student and I believed in him, but he stole my work **mutated** it."

"Who was this guy?" I pleaded. "And what did he want with Dad?"

"All you need to know right now is that this guy is **very dangerous**," said Grandma, putting her hand on my shoulder.

"And I'm afraid he's still up to no good ... **creating monsters.** I'm guessing he's after something only our town can give him."

"Something *Duck Creek* can give him?" said Kenny, pausing with a handful of popcorn halfway to his mouth.

Grandma continued. "For years there have been rumours of **a rare purple stone** found only in this region. The stone has a high amount of hypno-magnetic energy. To most people this would be useless, but if you know how to use the stone, it's very powerful."

Grandma rubbed her chin. "My guess is he's trying to drive everyone out of Duck Creek to get to it. He'll do **whatever** it takes."

"What does the stone look like?" I asked.

"It looks just like a plain rock, only it has tiny **flecks of purple triangles** in it." Grandma grabbed a pencil and began sketching on a pad. She drew a round, flat disc . . . just like the rock I'd thrown at the BUG OFF can in the woods!

"You've seen it?" asked Mum, when my eyes went wide.

"Yes!" I said. "I used it as **a ninja disc!**"

Grandma sat up. "Oh my! We have to move quickly!"

Grandma tapped away furiously on a keyboard. A screen blinked to life.

CLASSIFIED
Password: ✱ ✱ ✱ ✱ ✱ ✱ ✱ ✱

"What's this?" asked Kenny.

Grandma talked while she pressed different buttons. "I have access to a **secret network** available only to the special forces . . . it seems even the FBI is worried about this guy. He's been working on some crazy stuff for years and now he's created something **REALLY BAD.**"

Suddenly, a big headline popped up:

GIANT SPIDERS SPOTTED HIGH IN DUCK CREEK MOUNTAINS

"Our mountains," said Grandma, nodding in the direction of the rocky ridge looming over Duck Creek.

"Boys, these spiders are big and very deadly, just like the Tyranno-Spider you met today. But there isn't just one giant spider, there's **a whole gang** of them. Different species, too – big, strong tarantulas and trapdoor spiders that can leap entire buildings. They're mutations."

More giant spiders? **Gulp!**
Suddenly, I had an idea:

"Let's use your **ZAP-O-MATIC** to shrink them!" I said. "Get them down to their normal size!"

"Great idea!" said Grandma.

"OR . . ." started Kenny, "we can zap some pigeons to make **GIANT PIGEONS** and they'll just **eat** the spiders!"

"I . . . think we'll go with plan A," said Mum.

"OK," said Grandma. "I'll get the **ZAP-O-MATIC** ready tonight. The spiders are being controlled by a real bully, and they're probably going to attack really soon. Only someone with special powers will be able to stop them . . ."

Mum, Grandma, Kenny – everyone was looking at me.

They were counting on me. **Me.**

I felt woozy. What if I let everyone down?

I'd had a hard enough time battling **ONE** mutant spider, let alone a whole **army** of them!

SEVEN

I woke to a familiar **ringing** in my ears. At first I thought it was my alarm clock, but then I realized it was the high-pitched ringing I'd heard back in the woods. Right before the **Tyranno- Spider** attacked!

The spider army **was coming!**

I launched out of bed, flew down the stairs, and ran to get Grandma. To my surprise, she was already at the kitchen table fitting a shrunken **ZAP-O-MATIC** on to my backpack.

"They're coming!" I said. "I can hear them!"

Grandma ran to the window.

"There they are! They're heading for the town square!"

A sleepy-looking Kenny flicked on the TV . . .

MONSTER SPIDERS ON THE LOOSE!

"Hey, what happened to my cartoons?" whined Kenny.

"There's no time for that," I said. "We have **a serious pest problem** to deal with!"

At that moment, the sound of a helicopter **thundered** overhead and the ringing in my ears **grew louder**.

"Nelson, quick!" said Grandma.

She **threw** me the solar-powered shoes and the backpack. The ZAP-O-MATIC's hose and nozzle poked out of a pocket on the side.

Then Grandma pulled out one more thing. "Just like all the superheroes you've read about, you'll need a **disguise** so the bad guys can't come after you."

"That's OK, I can wear my hoodie again!"

"That won't **do**. Too many people have already seen you in that."

She handed me a long soccer sock with eyeholes cut out. **"A sock?!** This is my ninja disguise?!"

"Sorry, I didn't have much time," replied Grandma.

"This sock **stinks!**" said Kenny.

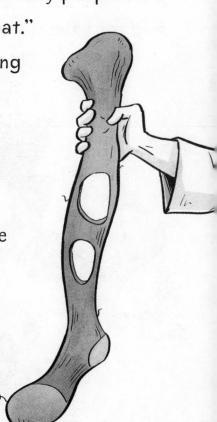

That was a **big** deal for Kenny, who'd happily wear the same underwear for a **month**.

Grandma shrugged. "Sorry, Nelson, like I said, I didn't have much time."

I strapped the sock **over my eyes** and tied it at the side.

Next, I tightened the **solar-powered shoes**, hoping they'd been improved since last time.

"**Go**," said Grandma. "We'll catch up!"

"But . . ." I stammered. I wanted to ask them . . . What if I couldn't do this ninja thing? There was **so** much responsibility.

Before I could utter another word, my shoes **flew me** out the front door!

I couldn't believe **how fast** I was going. **It felt awesome!** I was going to be in the town square in just seconds!

But then the sun slipped behind some clouds.

Suddenly, my feet **stopped** moving! **Uh-oh.**

Then, just as I'd expected, the shoes started running **backward** . . . I was heading back home!

"You're kidding, aren't you, Grandma?"
I muttered to myself. **"What am I going to do now?"**

Then I had an idea. The **heater torch** thing!

Worth a try.

I pulled it out of my backpack and flicked on the switch. I aimed it down at my shoes and . . .

I was off again!

Racing like a speeding **bullet** in the right direction!

There was absolute **CHAOS** in town. Mayor Brock and all these other people were wrapped in silk and dangling upside down from the top of our town hall.

A row of parked cars had been **crushed** by an enormous tarantula, and people were running and screaming all over the place.

Five giant black spiders were making their way across the car park to the supermarket.

As I fumbled for the **ZAP-O-MATIC** nozzle, one of the spiders turned and stared right at me.

It was so **big** and **hairy** and **gross** . . . and now it was heading my way!

UH-OH!

I wasn't ready for this!

Out of the chaos, Kenny emerged on his skateboard . . . eating an ice cream. He was holding a **HUGE** rubber flip-flop under his arm.

"Kenny? What are you doing?"

"I've brought **a giant sandal** to **squash the giant spiders!**"

"Well, you'd better get out of the way!
I'm not sure how to use this thing."

I aimed the laser beam at the giant black spider and **fired!**

ZAP!

My first shot missed and hit a garbage truck instead. It **shrank** to the size of a matchbox.

PiNG!

The spider kept coming!

I focused, aimed, and **fired** again. This time, the **glowing** blue beam was right on target, but just before impact, the spider jumped out of the way.

The laser beam **bounced** off a glass door and **whizzed** back our way, heading straight for Kenny!

It struck Kenny's ice cream just as he was about to take a bite. The ice cream shrank down to the size of a coin.

AH!

"Why does this keep happening to me?!" Kenny groaned.

My backpack started **beeping**. My batteries were low!

This meant I had only one shot left!

I looked over at the group of giant spiders in the supermarket car park. I had an idea.

"Kenny, I need you to get me some

BUG OFF. As much as you can fit in a shopping trolley!"

"I'm on it!" Kenny **jumped** on his skateboard and sped towards the store.

He skated **in** and **out** of the spiders' legs and into the supermarket.

I looked around, working out my plan. I had A **LOT** of massive spiders to round up.

The huge tarantula was thundering over to a couple of people in the park. Then I realized the people were **Sarah and her grandpa!** Her grandpa threw his walking stick right at the tarantula.

DONK!

Uh-oh! That was not a good move! The tarantula was **MAD!**

I quickly reached into my pack and pulled out **a ninja disc**. I threw it at the spider to distract it.

TING!

It worked! The spider turned and started heading towards me. Sarah and her grandpa were safe for now.

Suddenly, the loud whipping noise started again. **WHUP-WHUP-WHUP-WHUP-WHUP.**

Then the high-pitched sound.

All the spiders stopped and looked up at the red chopper. That maniac must have been controlling them with **sound waves**. Sound waves that *my* improved senses could pick up.

The trapdoor and black widow spiders **scuttled** towards the tarantula. They all seemed to be preparing to **attack** a group of old people.

"**INCOMING!**" screeched Kenny as he zipped down the pavement towards me, wheeling a shopping trolley filled with cans of BUG OFF.

YEAH!

"Good work, Kenny!"

I started piercing the cans with a ninja disc and they began to **fizz**.

"We need to lead them away from the old folks and back to the car park, where I can safely **blast** them all in one go! Follow me!"

I grabbed the shopping trolley and began to push it towards the spiders.

"Over here!" I shouted. "Come and get it!"

"Uh-oh," said Kenny as the spider horde crawled over to us.

"We have to move fast!" I yelled.

I rode the trolley like a scooter, speeding back to the car park. The BUG OFF spray fizzed and wafted out, drawing the spiders along.

"*Incy-wincy spiders,*" Kenny sang as he skated along behind me.

I pushed the trolley into the middle of the empty car park. The spiders jumped right over us to get to it.

"NOOOOOO!" boomed the voice from the sky. But his commands were

being ignored as the spiders pounced on
the trolley, devouring the bug spray.

"Stand back!" I yelled to Kenny. He
jumped behind me as I carefully aimed
and fired the ZAP-O-MATIC nozzle at
the group of spiders.

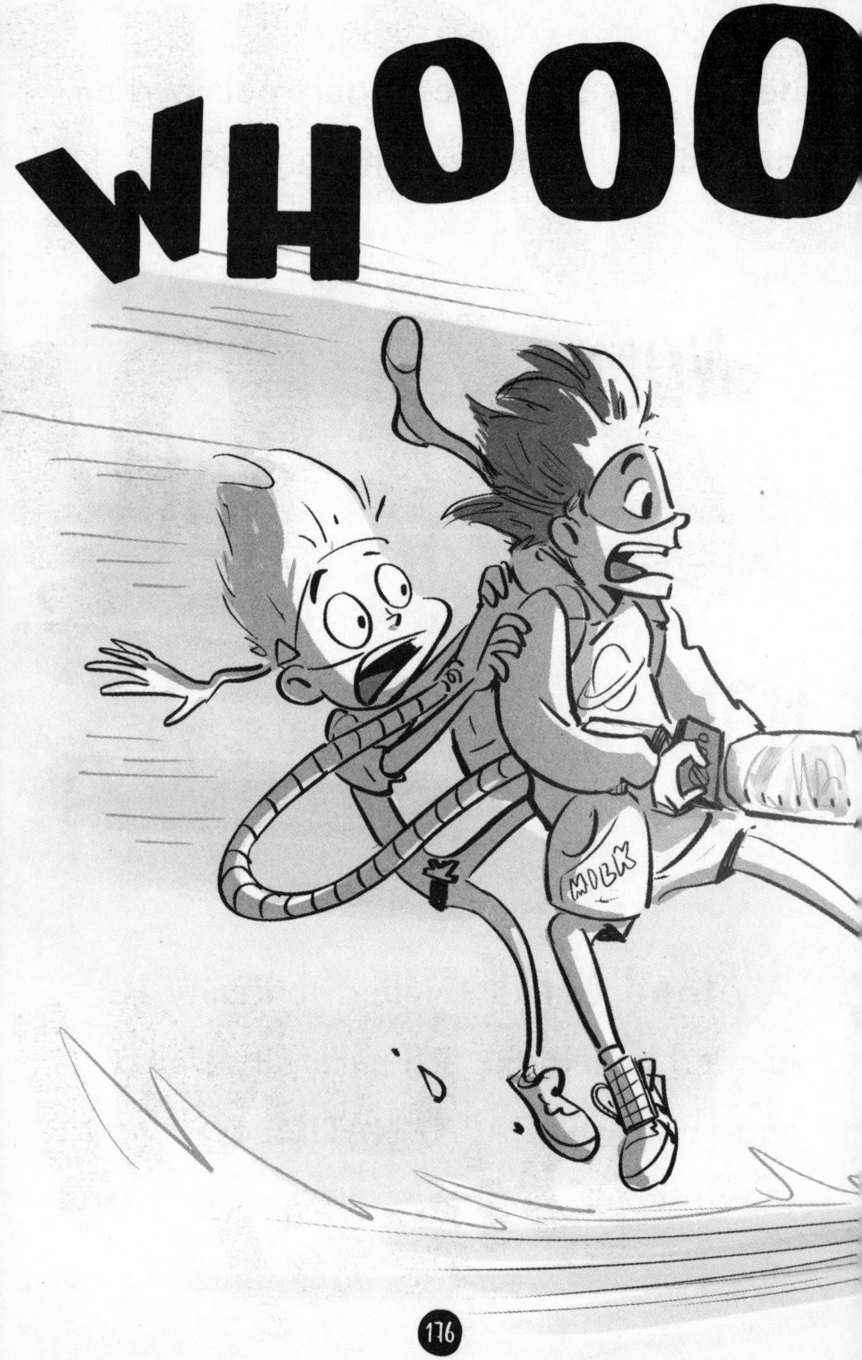
WHOOO
MOLK

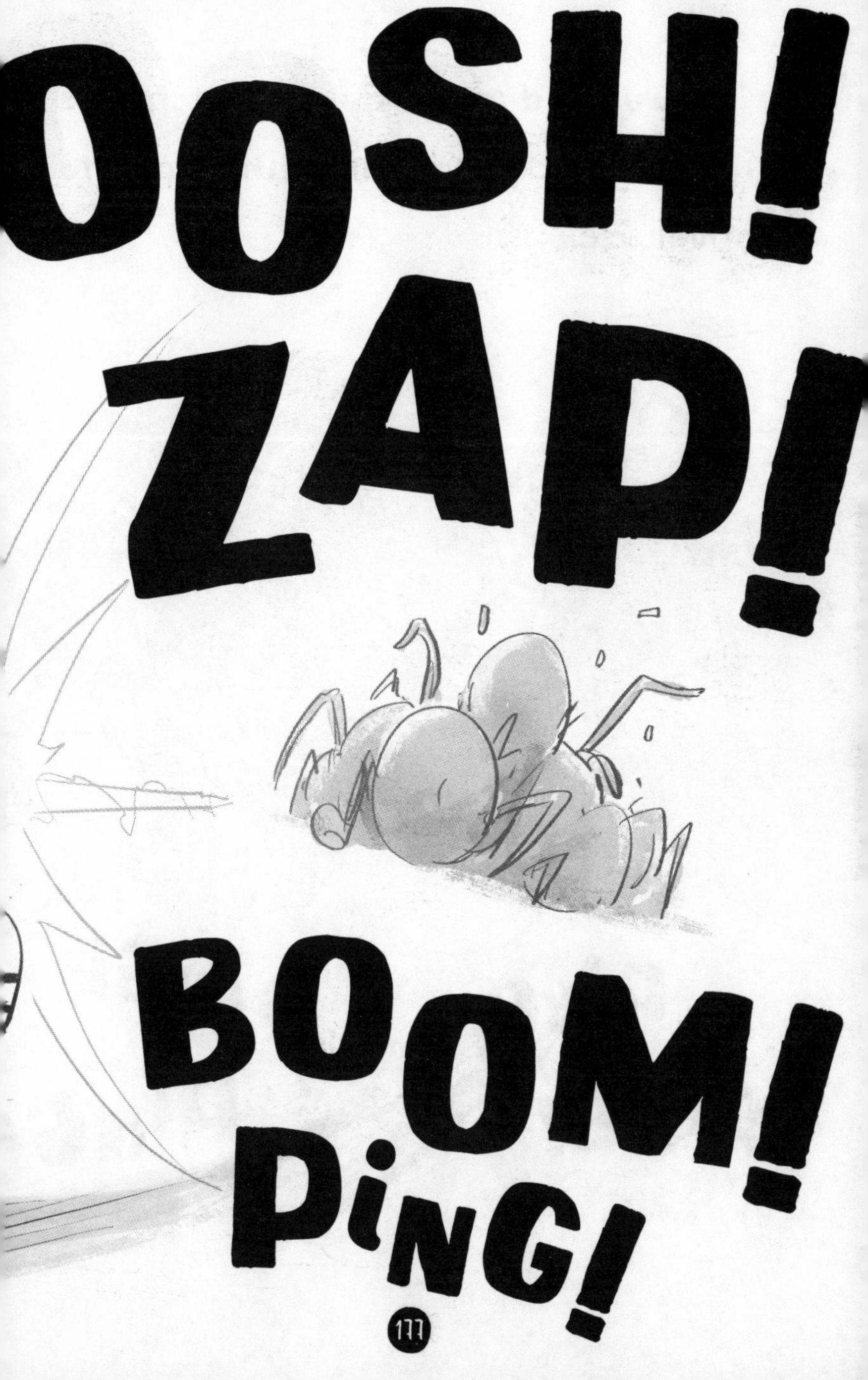
OOSH!
ZAP!
BOOM!
PiNG!

We watched as one by one the spiders **sizzled** and pinged, **shrinking** down to normal size.

"YOU DID IT!" yelled Kenny.
"WE DID IT!" I shouted.

We stared in amazement as all the little spiders scuttled away.

It was only then that I realized how exhausted I was.

Thank goodness it was all over!

At that moment, a **pesky** fly flew on to my face. I swatted it, but it hovered right in front of my eyes and then landed on my nose. My new and improved vision allowed me to see the creature clearly.

I couldn't believe it! It was the red chopper! Shrunken down like a tiny bug!

And for the first time, I saw the face behind the glass. A face so strangely familiar . . .

"You'll pay for this!" a shrill little voice screeched. Then the tiny chopper took off and disappeared into the sky.

EiGHT

Back home, Mum, Grandma, Kenny and I were celebrating our great victory over the monster spiders with a tray of hot chocolate and brownies.

I couldn't believe how far I'd come in my **ninja training** already . . . but something was still bothering me. I just couldn't put my finger on it.

"*Pleeeease*, Grandma," begged Kenny. "Let us use the ZAP-O-MATIC to make these brownies **bigger!**"

"I'm afraid not," said Grandma. "Remember, we have to use our power for the greater good. *Not* for brownies!"

"But it would be for the greater good of **my belly!**" argued Kenny.

At that moment, my dad's photo on the wall **caught my eye**.

I suddenly realized why the guy in the chopper had looked so **familiar**.

He was an angrier, wilder version of . . .

MY DAD!

WHAT THE?!

Something tells me this **ninja kid** thing is about to get a whole lot CRAZIER!

NiNJA KiD 2

COMING SOON!